Lily
and the
Yucky
Cookies

SEAN COVEY

Illustrated by Stacy Curtis

Ready-to-Read

Simon Spotlight
New York London Toronto Sydney New Delhi

To my amazing son Weston,
for listening to all my wild stories at night
—Sean Covey

For my sister, Shelley
—Stacy Curtis

SIMON SPOTLIGHT
An imprint of Simon & Schuster Children's Publishing Division
1230 Avenue of the Americas, New York, New York 10020
This Simon Spotlight edition May 2020
Copyright © 2013 by Franklin Covey Co.
All rights reserved, including the right of reproduction in whole or in part in any form.
SIMON SPOTLIGHT, READY-TO-READ, and colophon are registered trademarks of Simon & Schuster, Inc.
For information about special discounts for bulk purchases, please contact Simon & Schuster Special
Sales at 1-866-506-1949 or business@simonandschuster.com.
Manufactured in the United States of America 0420 LAK
2 4 6 8 10 9 7 5 3 1
Library of Congress Cataloging-in-Publication Data
Names: Covey, Sean, author. | Curtis, Stacy, illustrator.
Title: Lily and the yucky cookies / by Sean Covey ; illustrated by Stacy Curtis.
Description: Simon Spotlight edition. | New York : Simon Spotlight, 2020. | Series: The 7 habits of happy
kids ; 5 | Audience: Ages 5–7. | Summary: Lily Skunk bakes cookies for her friends without listening to
her father's instructions.
Identifiers: LCCN 2019041524 | ISBN 9781534444560 (paperback) | ISBN 9781534444577 (hardcover) |
ISBN 9781534444584 (eBook)
Subjects: CYAC: Listening—Fiction. | Baking—Fiction. | Skunks—Fiction.
Classification: LCC PZ7.C8343 Lil 2020 | DDC [E]–dc23
LC record available at https://lccn.loc.gov/2019041524

"Is it going to rain all day, Dad?"
asked Lily Skunk.
Lily Skunk was bored.
She and her friends had planned
to go to Fish-Eye Lake.
The rain washed out their plans.

"We can bake cookies instead.
It's a perfect rainy day treat,"
Lily's dad said.
Lily had watched Mom bake cookies
many, many times.
"I know exactly what to do,"
said Lily.

She climbed onto the step stool
and grabbed a big bowl.
Her dad said, "Well, let's check the
recipe just to be sure."

"First you have to mix two cups
of flour, a half cup of sugar,
and a pinch of . . . are you listening,
Lily?" asked Dad.

"Daaaad," said Lily. "I don't need a recipe. I know what I'm doing." "Be careful, Lily. You're moving awfully fast," her dad said.

"It's all right, Dad.
They'll be perfect."
Lily finished mixing.
She and her dad put the cookie
dough on the baking sheet.

Lily put on oven mitts
and carried the sheet to the oven.
Then her dad helped her put
the cookies in the oven.

Before long the cookies were done
and had cooled off.
Just then Lily's brother, Stink,
spotted the sun coming out.
"You can go to Fish-Eye Lake now,"
he said.

Lily gave Stink a cookie and
raced for the door.
Stink nibbled on it and said,
"But, Lily, these cookies are . . ."
Lily didn't listen as she rushed off
to Fish-Eye Lake.

Lily rowed her boat
to Goat Island
in the lake.
She met her friends,
who were swimming.
She was excited to share
the cookies she had baked.

"Hi, everyone!
I brought cookies!
I baked them myself.
I hope you like them,"
said Lily.
"Oh, Lily, those look delectable!"
said Sophie.

Everyone swam to the shore
and took a cookie.
"Yuck! They taste like salt,"
said Jumper.
"I think I'm going to throw up,"
said Pokey.

"Lily, the cookies are kind of gross,"
said Tagalong Allie.
Lily felt awful.
She didn't know what went wrong.
So she went home.

At home, Lily found her dad.
"Dad, nobody liked my cookies.
Allie said they were gross, and
Pokey almost threw up.
So I dumped them all in the
garbage," said Lily.

"It's okay, Lily. We can make more. You just need to listen next time. You don't have to follow the recipe exactly, but you want to make sure you understand every step before you get started," said her dad.

Lily stopped and listened.
She did not want to rush anymore.

She wanted to follow the recipe
and make yummy cookies.
She asked, "Can we bake cookies
again? I promise, promise, promise
that I'll listen this time."

After dinner, Lily and her dad
went back to the kitchen
to make more cookies.
Lily listened as her dad read
the whole recipe aloud.

She followed each step, except one.
She used chocolate chips
instead of raisins!
Stink tried to help too,
but he kept eating
all the chocolate chips.

The next day Lily went to the park.
She had a new batch of cookies
for her friends.
"These are much better," said Lily.
But no one wanted to try them.
"I'm not going to go first,"
said Jumper.

Pokey did not move from the swing.
Finally Allie said, "I'll try one."
Everyone watched as Allie
slowly picked up one
and took a small bite.

"Yup, yup, yup.
These are the best cookies ever, Lily!"
Everyone started grabbing
and eating cookies.
Pretty soon they were all gone.

Jumper loved Lily's cookies so much, he could not stop jumping around.

Goob could not stop smiling.
"Those cookies are
so yummy for my tummy,"
he said.

"What's in them?"
asked Pokey.
"Well . . . ," Lily said,
"the secret ingredient is listening."

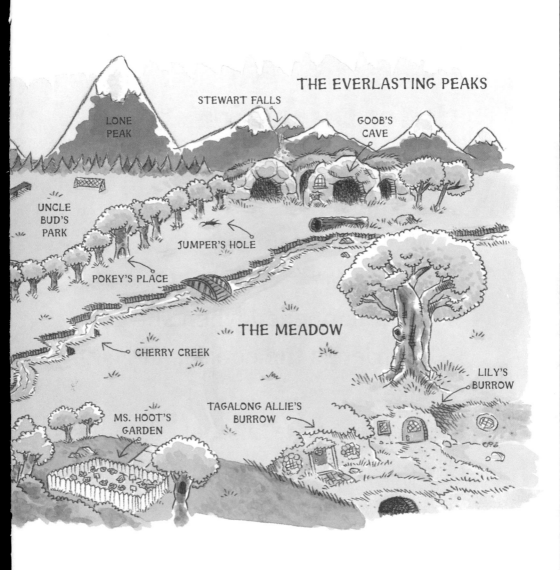

Up for Discussion

1. What did Lily do wrong while making cookies?
2. Why didn't Lily pay attention to her father?
3. What happened when she gave her friends the cookies at Fish-Eye Lake?
4. The next time Lily baked cookies, what did she do differently? What did her friends think about the new batch of cookies?
5. Why is it important to listen?

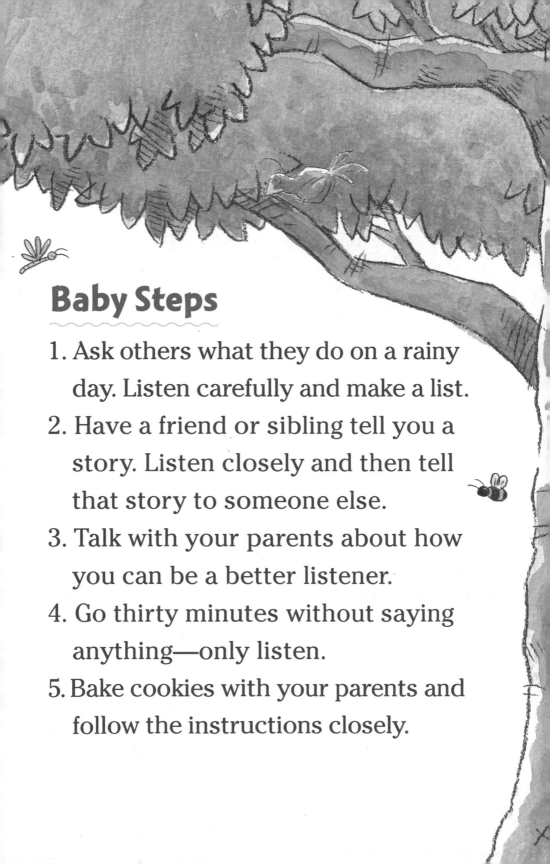

Baby Steps

1. Ask others what they do on a rainy day. Listen carefully and make a list.
2. Have a friend or sibling tell you a story. Listen closely and then tell that story to someone else.
3. Talk with your parents about how you can be a better listener.
4. Go thirty minutes without saying anything—only listen.
5. Bake cookies with your parents and follow the instructions closely.

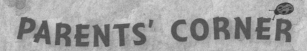

PARENTS' CORNER

HABIT ⑤ —Seek First to Understand, Then to Be
Understood: *Listen Before You Talk*

As Lily had to learn the hard way, seeking first to understand, or listening, is the secret ingredient of life. In general, there is way too much talking and way too little listening going on. Like Lily, we have a tendency to think we know it all, to rush in, to fix things up with good advice. We too often fail to read directions, to diagnose, to truly understand another person's point of view.

Seeking first to understand is a correct principle in all areas of life. A good writer will understand his audience before writing a paper. A good doctor will diagnose before she prescribes. A careful mother will understand her child before evaluating or judging. An effective teacher will assess the needs of his class before teaching.

In this story, Lily thought she knew it all and didn't take the time to listen. As a result, her cookies were yucky. When she took the time to listen and follow a recipe, the cookies were "yummy for my tummy," as Goob put it. And that's how it is in life, too. Listening takes time. It also produces a great batch of cookies. And it doesn't take anywhere near as much time as it takes to back up and correct misunderstandings when you're already miles down the road, to redo, to live with unexpressed and unsolved problems, to deal with the result of not giving people what they want most, which is simply to be understood.

Let us always remember that we have two ears and one mouth and we should use them accordingly.